Welcome to ALADDIN

If you are looking for f...
with colorful characters, lots of kid-friendly
humor, easy-to-follow action, entertaining
story lines, and lively illustrations, then
ALADDIN QUIX is for you!

But wait, there's more!

If you're also looking for stories with
tables of contents; word lists; about-the-
book questions; 64, 80, or 96 pages; short
chapters; short paragraphs; and large fonts,
then **ALADDIN QUIX** is *definitely* for you!

ALADDIN QUIX: The next step between ready
to reads and longer, more challenging chapter
books, for readers five to eight years old.

Read more ALADDIN QUIX books!

By Stephanie Calmenson

Our Principal Is a Frog!

Our Principal Is a Wolf!

Our Principal's in His Underwear!

Our Principal Breaks a Spell!

Our Principal's Wacky Wishes!

Our Principal Is a Spider!

Our Principal Is a Scaredy-Cat!

Our Principal Is a Noodlehead!

The Adventures of Allie and Amy
By Stephanie Calmenson and Joanna Cole

Book 1: *The Best Friend Plan*

Book 2: *Rockin' Rockets*

Book 3: *Stars of the Show*

Book 4: *Costume Parade*

HARVEY HAMMER

New Shark in Town

BY
Davy Ocean

ILLUSTRATED BY
Aaron Blecha

ALADDIN QUIX

New York London Toronto Sydney New Delhi

ALADDIN QUIX
Simon & Schuster Children's Publishing Division
1230 Avenue of the Americas, New York, New York 10020
First Aladdin QUIX paperback edition May 2022
Text copyright © 2022 by Working Partners Limited
Illustrations copyright © 2022 by Aaron Blecha
New Shark in Town is a Working Partners book.
Also available in an Aladdin QUIX hardcover edition.
All rights reserved, including the right of reproduction in whole or in part in any form.
ALADDIN and the related marks and colophon are trademarks of Simon & Schuster, Inc.
For information about special discounts for bulk purchases, please contact
Simon & Schuster Special Sales at 1-866-506-1949 or business@simonandschuster.com.
The Simon & Schuster Speakers Bureau can bring authors to your live event.
For more information or to book an event contact the Simon & Schuster Speakers
Bureau at 1-866-248-3049 or visit our website at www.simonspeakers.com.
Designed by Karin Paprocki
The illustrations for this book were rendered digitally.
The text of this book was set in Archer Medium.
Manufactured in the United States of America 0322 OFF
2 4 6 8 10 9 7 5 3 1
Library of Congress Control Number 2021946000
ISBN 9781534455122 (hc)
ISBN 9781534455115 (pbk)
ISBN 9781534455139 (ebook)

Cast of Characters

Harvey Hammer: Young hammerhead shark

Squiddy: Harvey's inkpot

Dad Hammer: Father of Hettie, Harvey, and Finn

Paul: Harvey's pencil fish

Finn: Harvey's baby brother

Mom Hammer, aka Hanna: Chief of police; mother of Hettie, Harvey, and Finn

Snakey: Harvey's ruler

Eric: Harvey's erazor clam

Hettie: Harvey's older sister

Growler: The Hammers' dogfish

Flash: Turtle classmate

Spike: Puffer fish classmate and Harvey's enemy

Rocky: Barnacle classmate and Spike's best friend

Bluey: Whalebus driver

Pearl: Racing clam classmate

Ms. Lumpy: Harvey's teacher

Sandy: Sand shark classmate

Connie: Crab classmate

Principal T. Una: School principal

Dr. Pierce Puffer Fish: Spike's father

Contents

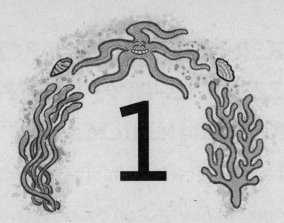

1

First Day, Worst Day

King Krusher, the Super Crime-Fighting Crab, and his sidekick, Hammer-Boy, were dodging bolts of electricity.

FZZZZZZZZZZZZZZ ZZTTTTTTTTT . . .

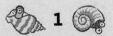

KER-CLACK. KER-CLACK. ZZZZZZ-TTTTT-FFFFF-ZAMMMMMMMM...

I looked down at the *King Krusher versus Dr. Eel-O-Stun* comic I'd been drawing. Dr. Eel-O-Stun, the baddest of bad guys in all the ocean, fired the bolts. He was on the steps outside the Sand-Bank—which he'd just robbed of A MILLION CLAM$....

ZAP. FZZZZZZZZZTTT.

One of the electric bolts was headed for Hammer-Boy.

What was our hero going to do...?

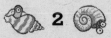 2

"**Harvey**! For the last time, please put that pencil fish *down* and get ready for *school.*"

PLAPAPAPAPAPLAP . . . SPLAT . . .

Squiddy the inkpot had been so **startled** by **Dad**'s voice that a huge **blot** of ink had popped out of his bottom onto the page. And **Paul** the pencil fish had scribbled over it in fright.

I turned toward Dad. **"Dad, now my comic is ruined!"**

Dad was holding my baby brother, **Finn**, out in front of him, as if Finn were about to explode from both ends. Half of Dad's hammerhead was coated in white, stinky baby throw-up.

 5

"Sorry about that, Son," said Dad. "But it's your first day at Kelpementary School, and the whalebus is almost here. If you're not on that bus, **Mom** will have both our fins."

We used to live in Shark Point but moved to Coral Cove because Mom got an important new job. She had already left for work earlier this morning. I wasn't about to tell my dad, but I felt pretty scared to be starting a new school.

Yes, my parents are sharks. So am I. A hammerhead. That means

 **6**

I have a head shaped like a hammer. I don't know how weird your Leggy-Air-Breather head is, but mine is pretty weird. Luckily for me, it's only the second-weirdest shark head in the sea.

GOBLIN
Shark

HAMMER HEAD
Shark

SAW
Shark

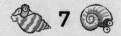

List of Weird Shark Heads

· Goblin sharks. They could win gold, silver, *and* bronze in the Strange O-swim-pics. They can push their jaws outside their mouths when they bite. *ICK.*

· Hammerheads. That's us.

· Saw sharks. Their noses are so sharp and *toothy,* they could eat lunch and build a table at the same time.

"I don't want to have to tell you again, Harvey," Dad said in his mega-serious voice. "Put away your things. **NOW.**"

"Okay," I said, **clenching** my jaw. I opened my pencil case so Paul and Squiddy could swim inside. Squiddy still looked shaken. I hoped he didn't poop all over **Snakey**, my sea snake ruler, and **Eric**, my erazor clam.

I wasn't even at school yet, and my day had gotten off to an awful start. Could it get any worse?

 **9**

2

Pacific-fier Panic

"**Hey!** Let's get a move on, Harvey."

I turned around and gave a **snarl**.
Hettie, my older sister, **barged** past.

I'm only a young hammerhead, so
my shark-snarl is more like a goofy
grin. It makes Hettie laugh in my face.

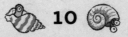

As usual, Hettie was *totally* ready for school. She is never late and always has her bag packed. She was carrying her sea bass guitar under her fin like she was a member of a famous pop group rather than a fish signing up for a Kelpementary School band.

It was her first day of middle school, but she was as cool as a sea cucumber.

I was just about to give Hettie a second snarl when a **wriggling** baby was **plonked** into my fins.

"Hold him, Harvey," Dad said,

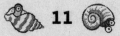

ducking under the kitchen table. "Finn's dropped his Pacific-fier."

Dad's tail flapped as he searched. His head bobbed up at the other side of the table.

"I can't find it!"

Finn began to cry.

"It's okay," Dad said as my baby brother cried louder. Finn turned grouchier than a great white if he didn't have his Pacific-fier.

"Harvey," Dad said in a panic. **"Hammervision, please!"**

Hammerheads have a sixth sense

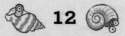

that allows us to search for **signals** in the water to locate stuff. I have the best Hammervision in the family. It's the one thing I can do even better than Hettie can.

PING. PING. PING.

I started looking for signals. The kitchen turned electric green in my

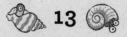

head. The beeps and blips zipped around, bouncing off everything.

Bingo. The Pacific-fier.

"It's in **Growler**'s mouth," I said.

Growler is our grumpy old dog-fish. He thinks anything that floats onto the floor is his.

PING. PING. PING.

I could see that Growler's cheeks were **bulging**. The Pacific-fier was scrunched up under his tongue.

Dad had to chase Growler five times around the kitchen to get it back.

Finn was so happy I'd found the Pacific-fier that he thanked me by throwing up on my school shirt.

"Finn!" I howled.

Hettie screamed with laughter.

Finn let out a loud **BURP**.

"The whalebuses are here," Dad said, taking Finn from my fins and looking out the window.

"I can't go to school covered in baby shark goop." I groaned. "And my other shirts are still packed away."

"You need to get on that bus," said Dad. And he pushed me and Hettie out the door.

It turned out my day could get worse, after all.

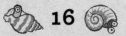

3

Rocky Ride

Hettie swished to her middle school whalebus, and I zoomed onto mine.

Although it was the first day back for everyone else, it was my first day at *everything*. I'd never even seen the school before, and all the

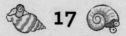

kids and squids were strangers to me.

The two whalebuses started their journeys to school. Feeling all funny in my tummy, I plopped down in a seat next to a turtle shell.

I couldn't see the turtle's head, legs, or arms. But I heard him whining. I knocked on the shell with my hammerhead. "Hello? Anyone home?"

The turtle's head came out of one hole, and a clawed flipper came out of another. The flipper clamped over

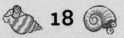

his nose. "Can you please do something about the stink?" he asked.

I spotted a little of Finn's goop on my sleeve and rubbed it away the best I could.

The turtle took down his claw and smiled. "Thanks," he said. "I'm **Flash.**"

"Harvey Hammer," I replied, holding out a fin. "I'm new."

But instead of shaking my fin, Flash popped back inside his shell.

Just then, a voice screeched, **"INCOMING!"**

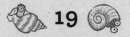

A finball zoomed past my head and bounced off Flash's shell.

"Ouch!" the shell echoed. "That rattled my beak."

The finball rebounded onto a big **barnacle**, who hit it toward a large, spiny puffer fish. "Catch it,

Spike!" yelled the barnacle.

The puffer fish batted the finball back to the barnacle. "All yours, **Rocky!**"

The finball spun through the air and hit the back of **Bluey** the whale-bus driver's head.

"No finball on the bus," **rumbled** Bluey. He pulled up against the sandwalk outside school, and the bus started to empty out.

I don't think I'd ever been more glad to get to school. Whalebus trips back at my old school had *never*

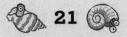

been like this. *What else is going to happen today?* I wondered.

Flash's head came out of his shell. "Have Rocky and Spike gone?"

I nodded. "Yes."

Flash looked relieved. "I don't like playing finball with those guys. They are so rough."

"I don't even like finball that much," I said. "I like drawing comics. One day I'm going to be a famous comic book artist."

"That's cool," said Flash. "I'm going to be a famous racing clam driver."

 22

As we were swimming off the bus, a voice stopped us.

"Here's your helmet, Flash," said a sleek clam. She was holding a striped helmet. "My mom put the six on it, just like you asked."

A smile spread over Flash's beak as he grabbed the helmet. **"That's perfect!"** He screwed the helmet onto his head. "How does it look?"

"Great," I said.

"Harvey, this is **Pearl**," said Flash. "Not only is she my friend but she's also my racing clam. She's

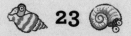 23

the speediest shellfish around."

I'd heard of racing clams, but I'd never seen one up close before. Pearl looked amazingly powerful and speedy. As her driver, Flash would have to be really good at balancing.

Pearl pushed out her exhaust tubes and began pumping bubbly jets of water through them. "Come on, Flash," she said. "A quick practice before attendance."

Flash leaped onto her back and balanced like he was on a surfboard. They sped off, looking supercool.

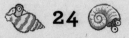

"See you in class, Harvey," Pearl called back.

And I was alone.

On my first day.

Maybe I should turn around and go home to my throwing-up baby brother, I thought.

4

Class Dis-fished

CRUNCH-CH-CH-CH!

Oh no!

Colored pencils were flying every-

where. I had swum into my new class

and smacked into a bookshelf.

Every fish eye and eyestalk in

the class was suddenly looking at me. I could feel my hammer turning red. I heard a couple of squids giggling.

"Now, everyone, settle down," said a lady sea cucumber. "It's Harvey's first day at our school. I'm sure you all remember how scary it was on *your* first day, hmm? Let's be more welcoming."

The sea cucumber helped me gather up the pencils. It probably only took a few seconds, but it felt like three hours.

"I'm your teacher, **Ms. Lumpy.** I'm sure you'll fit right in, but let's give you a hammerhead start."

Ms. Lumpy began telling me the names of the other kids and squids.

List of My Classmates

- Flash the turtle
- Pearl the racing clam
- Spike the puffer fish
- Rocky the barnacle
- Sandy the sand shark
- Connie the crab

· lots more kids and squids whose names I forgot
because it was my first day and I was really
nervous, but you get the idea

When Ms. Lumpy finished telling
me their names, I looked around the
class. Most of the kids smiled at me.
But Spike and Rocky weren't smiling.

"The new shark smells of baby
goop," I heard Spike whisper to
Rocky.

Sigh.

Be the bigger fish, Harvey. That's
what my mom would say.

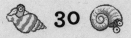 **30**

"And stop looking at me like that," said Spike.

"I can't help that my eyes are on the sides of my head, Spike," I said. But I turned my head sideways so I wasn't looking at him.

"Face the front, please, Harvey," called Ms. Lumpy. "It's time to start our first math lesson."

Great. I'd knocked over a pile of stuff and been told I stank of goop, and now Ms. Lumpy had singled me out. Was school over yet?

Luckily, the rest of the morning

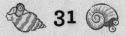 31

went **surprisingly** well. I knew that seven times seven was forty-nine, how to spell "octopus," and that some jellyfish can glow in the dark.

Right before our lunch break, Spike turned around to me. "Hey, goggly," he whispered. "We're playing finball at recess. The other team needs one more player."

"Sure, I'll play," I told him.

He puffed up so his spines poked toward me like sharp needles. "But just because you're new in Coral Cove, don't think I'm going to let you win."

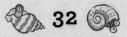

"Haha," I laughed nervously. "See you at recess."

What had I gotten myself into? I stink at finball.

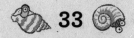

5

Squid Goals

Zhuuupppppp!

The finball whizzed by my hammer. It missed me by a shark's tooth.

Only minutes before this I had been picked for Rocky's team—so had Flash and **Sandy**. The game

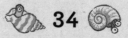

had started with a toot from Pearl's
referee whistle. Spike's first kick
had almost taken my hammer off.

Spike had made himself the goalie
for his team because, he announced,
"I'm the best goalie this school has
ever had. I never let *anything* past
me."

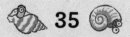

At first I thought this was just Spike bragging. But every time one of our players got near him, they finned the finball right over the top of the goal.

Before we knew it, our team was losing 2–0. And the kids, squids, and jellyfish in the crowd were cheering hard.

Connie was waving her claw, trying to make us take the finball upfield.

Sandy leaped and dorsal-finned the ball toward Flash, who beaked it so that it almost hit Pearl.

I was near the sideline. *Please*

 36

don't pass to me, please don't pass to me, I thought.

But then Connie saw me and blasted the finball right toward my tail.

I rolled forward **awkwardly**. Then I splashed backward. Then, just when I thought I was going to miss, I whacked the ball with my hammer toward Flash. . . .

The finball whistled out of bounds.

"Hahahahahaha," Spike howled. "Harvey couldn't hit a reef with a basking shark."

Then, luckily for us, Pearl called,
"TIME-OUT!"

Each team swam over to their goal. We **huddled** around Rocky.

"Yes, we're down by two fin-goals. But, Harvey, you've got a great head for heading the finball," Rocky said. "And don't listen to Spike. He's just being annoying."

That made me feel so much better. Rocky might have been one of Spike's best friends, but that didn't mean he was horrible too.

"TIME-IN!" Pearl yelled.

PHWEEEEEEEEEEE! went her whistle, and I was off.

After all the disasters that had happened on my very first day:

- Finn's throw-up
- a stinky bus ride
- and knocking pencils all over the class . . .

Scoring a goal was going to make me feel a whole lot better.

I finned the ball from under Sandy's flipper.

"Harvey . . . ," called Flash.

I nose-spun the finball over Rocky's shell.

"Wait!" shouted Flash.

Spike **crouched** in the goal, blowing on his fintips as I sped toward him.

I swerved around a leaping lobster. I smacked the finball with my tail.

I guess I wasn't so stinky after all.

Spike had *no* chance.

The finball was going to power into the top corner of the net. I was going to score....

"Harvey!" screamed Flash. "Puffer fish can..."

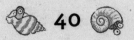

Spike the puffer fish puffed himself up. And his spines stuck out like a thousand porcupine fish swimming in **formation**.

WHUUUUUUFFFFFOPPP!

The finball hit Spike's spikes and burst open with a huge **POP**.

Tatters of the finball hung on Spike, fluttering in the current.

Spike smiled.

Everyone else groaned.

"That was our last finball. And you, Harvey Hammer, burst it!" Sandy yelled.

Which wasn't really fair, but I could see why she'd said it.

Pearl blew her whistle. **"Spike's team wins 2–0!"**

I followed the others back into school. No one was laughing; they

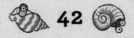

were just looking at me like they
wished they'd never met me.

It was game over. If only it could
be *day* over too.

6

Surprise

When we came in from recess, Ms. Lumpy made an announcement. "We have a surprise assembly for our first day back. Please line up and follow me down the hall."

My hammer **perked** up at this. An

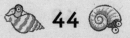

assembly sounded much more fun than schoolwork.

I really *needed* some fun right then, because every time I looked, someone was whispering behind their fin and looking at me like I'd gooped in their lunch box.

The class formed a line and began to swim down to the assembly cave. Flash swam next to me, and I could hear Spike snickering somewhere behind us.

"He couldn't score even if the goal were thirty fathoms wide and I

were back in my seabed," Spike said,
and the kids and squids around him
laughed.

My hammerhead grew hot. I knew
he was talking about me.

I looked at Flash to see if he'd heard, but the turtle was just staring ahead. I could tell he was still sad about the burst finball.

Up on the stage were Ms. Lumpy and **Principal T. Una**. The principal was a large, kindly fish with a pair of fish spectacles balanced on his nose.

"Well, kid-squids and fish-fry," he said once everyone had settled down. "It's our first day back at school, and we've got a special treat—two Sea-I-P guests to talk to you about their jobs.

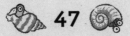 47

First up is the father of your class-mate Spike—**Dr. Pierce Puffer Fish.**"

From the corner of my hammer, I saw Spike puff up with pride.

"Wow! Brilliant! Amazing!" said many of the kids and squids. Dr. Pierce swam onto the stage in his white coat with a stethoscope hanging around his neck and a doctor's identification tag.

Squids were turning to Spike. "Your dad's a doctor? That is so cool."

Great. Spike had made me look like a clown fish on the finball field,

and now he was also getting all the compliments from the class.

"And here to talk about her new job in Coral Cove," said Principal T. Una, "is our new chief of police, Hanna Hammer."

My eyes bulged like expanding jellyfish, my hammer felt like it was spiraling, and if my tummy had had fins, it would have punched the air. My mom, wearing her blue uniform, her coral shield glinting, was swimming up to join Dr. Pierce.

I told you my mom's job was important.

"Double wow."

"Mega amazing."

"Super brilliant."

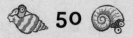

The kids and squids around me cheered and fin-plauded. I suddenly felt ninety fathoms tall.

I looked at Spike, who wasn't so puffed full of pride as he'd been before.

That showed him.

My day was finally getting good.

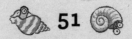

7

In Shame

Dr. Pierce began to speak first. "I always wanted to be a doctor. It's one of the best jobs in the sea. If you study hard, you too could be a doctor like me. Helping other fish can be such fun."

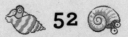

All the schoolsquids were listening carefully. I could see in their faces that they were really impressed.

If I twisted my hammer a little, I could also see that Spike's pride was puffing him back up again. His spines were starting to show around his body.

"The great thing about being a puffer fish and a doctor is that when it comes to giving fish their shots, it's easier than ever." Dr. Pierce explained as he puffed out his

spines. "I just dip a **sterilized** spine into the medicine bottle, suck the medicine up, and in it goes."

Everyone said, **"Oooooooh!"**

"You can give the shot into pretty much any muscle in the body, but the best muscle is in … the bottom."

A few people in the audience giggled.

Dr. Pierce pointed to a chart. "Now, of course babies need a lot of shots and checkups. If you all look at this picture here . . ."

He flipped the chart open, and

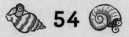

there was a picture of Spike as a
baby, drooling and wearing a huge
diaper.

The assembly began to howl and
laugh, giggle and hoot.

As I watched, Spike got redder and redder and **deflated** with

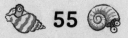

embarrassment. Hiding his face with his fins, he swam under the seats and out of the assembly cave on a tide of shame.

Well, now Spike finally knew what I'd felt like when I'd burst the finball on him.

Served him right.

Dr. Pierce finished his talk to waves of fin-plauding.

Now it was my mom's turn.

I floated back in my chair, ready for the fin-plause and the con-gratulations about how she was a

brilliant chief of police.

"It's funny you should talk about getting shots, Dr. Pierce," Mom began. "Because when my son Harvey over there . . ."

Mom pointed a fin at me.

"Needed his shots for our over-seas vacation just last year . . ."

Gulp. *Don't go there, Mom.*

"Every night of the week, before bed . . ."

She's going there.

"He threw up."

I now turned much redder than Spike had.

And if the laughing from the assembly was any harder or louder than it had been for Spike, I didn't stop to find out. I was pumping my tail and heading for the door so fast,

 58

my hammers were bent back over my ears.

I didn't want anyone to see how embarrassed I was by what my mom had said. So when I zoomed into the schoolyard, I headed for the nearest seaweed bush and dived beneath it. I buried my hammer in the cool **fronds** and hoped my tail wasn't showing.

"Hey. This is my place."

I opened my eyes. There in front of me, just as miserable, was Spike.

I looked at his red face.

He looked at my red hammer.

"Parents!"

We both said it at the same time. And both understood why we'd said it.

"Why do parents have to keep showing off?" Spike said.

"Why can't parents behave themselves?" I replied.

At that, we both laughed.

"I guess you're not so bad after all," Spike said when we'd finished laughing.

"I suppose you aren't either,"
I said. I stuck out my fin. "Fin
bump?"

Spike hesitated for a moment,
then bumped fins with me. "You

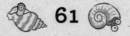

wanna come kick a finball around with me until assembly's fin-ished?"

"Yeah," I said. "And then after, I can show you my latest comic book."

It had been a long first day. A weird, embarrassing, long first day. I was glad it was over.

I couldn't wait to get home and finish my King Krusher comic. At least I kind of knew how that story would end.

° ° °

 **62**

FZZZZZZZZTTTTTTTT...

Hammer-Boy ducked as Dr. Eel-O-Stun's electric bolt shot toward him.

But as Hammer-Boy looked up, he saw that the bolt wasn't meant for him at all. It was heading for a different target.

A huge shadow passed over them both, turning the water cold.

The bolt sizzled on ... and hit the shadow right on the backside.

"OOOOOOOOWWWWWW," the shadow boomed in a voice that shook the ocean.

 63

The huge shadow came into a patch of light from the surface. Hammer-Boy saw that it belonged to Octopus-Prime, a super villain even more evil than Dr. Eel-O-Stun.

The electric shock had made Octopus-Prime's beak fly open. King Krusher fell out of his mouth.

"Thanks, Dr. Eel-O-Stun," said King Krusher. "You saved me from being crabnapped."

Hammer-Boy was amazed. Two enemies shaking claws and tails.

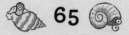 65

"Are we forming a crime-fighting trio?" Hammer-Boy asked.

"I wouldn't go that far," Dr. Eel-O-Stun said. "I am evil, after all. But I'll help you catch that eight-legged slippery customer."

"Then let's get Octopus-Prime before he gets away," Hammer-Boy roared. "He's no match for the three of us."

And do you know what?

He wasn't.

Word List

awkwardly (AW•kwurd•lee):
Clumsily, not gracefully

barged (BARJD): Moved clumsily, without thinking

barnacle (BAR•nih•kull): A sea animal that attaches itself to rocks, the bottom of ships, and other objects

blot (BLAHT): A spot or stain

bulging (BUHL•jing): Swelling or pushing out

 **67**

clenching (KLEN•ching): Closing tightly

crouched (KROWCHT): Lowered the body by bending the legs

deflated (dee•FLAY•ted): Got smaller by letting air escape

formation (for•MAY•shun): In a specific order

fronds (FRAHNDS): Large leaves

huddled (HUH•duld): Crowded together

perked (PURKD): Became more cheerful

plonked (PLAWNKD): Set down suddenly

referee (reh•fuh•REE): An official who manages how a game is played

rumbled (RUM•buld): Said in a low rolling tone

signals (SIG•nuhls): Ways that information can be sent or received

snarl (SNAHRL): A growl

startled (STAR•tuld): Suddenly surprised or frightened

sterilized (STARE•uh•lized): Freed of dirt and germs

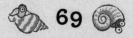

surprisingly (sir•PRY•zing•lee):

Unexpectedly

wriggling (RIH•guh•ling):

Twisting from side to side

 70

Questions

1. What did Finn do to Harvey before Harvey left the house?
2. Was Harvey nervous to start a new school? Was his older sister, Hettie?
3. Who is the hero of Harvey's comic book?
4. What did Dr. Pierce do that embarrassed Spike? Do you think that would embarrass you?

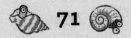

5. What kind of creature is Flash? What does he want to be when he grows up? What do want to be when you grow up?